When Bholu Came Back

STORY Kavitha Punniyamurthi

PICTURES Niloufer Wadia

To my son Sai, who came five months before the book did. – Kavitha

When Bholu Came Back (English)

ISBN 978-93-5046-793-0
© text Kavitha Punniyamurthi
© illustrations Niloufer Wadia
First published in India, 2016
Reprinted in 2017

Published by
Tulika Publishers, 24/1 Ganapathy Colony Third Street, Teynampet, Chennai 600 018, India
email tulikabooks@vsnl.com website www.tulikabooks.com

Printed and bound by
Sudarsan Graphics, 27 Neelakanta Mehta Street, T. Nagar, Chennai 600 017, India

Beni Ram was sad. He had just sold his camel Bholu at the Camel Fair.

Beni Ram stopped to shake the sand out of his holey shoes.

Wait, what was that sound?

Shlop-shlop! Shlop-shlop! Shlop-shlop!

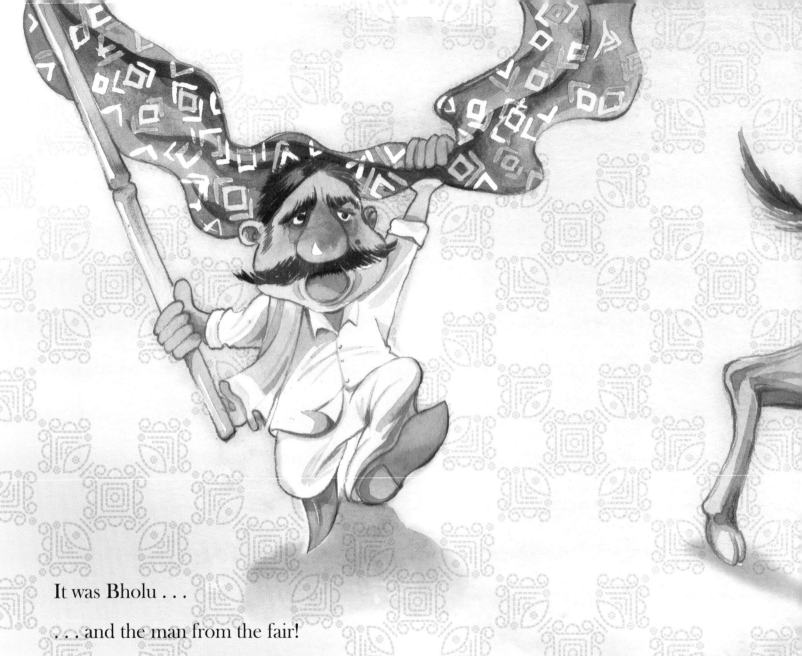

It was Bholu . . .

. . . and the man from the fair!

"STOP!" yelled the camel-buyer, running after
Bholu, waving his turban.

"Arrey, Bholiya!" cried Beni Ram. "You've come back? AGAIN!"

"Graa-aaa-aaa-ooo-oon!"

Bholu gave his old master a loving lick.

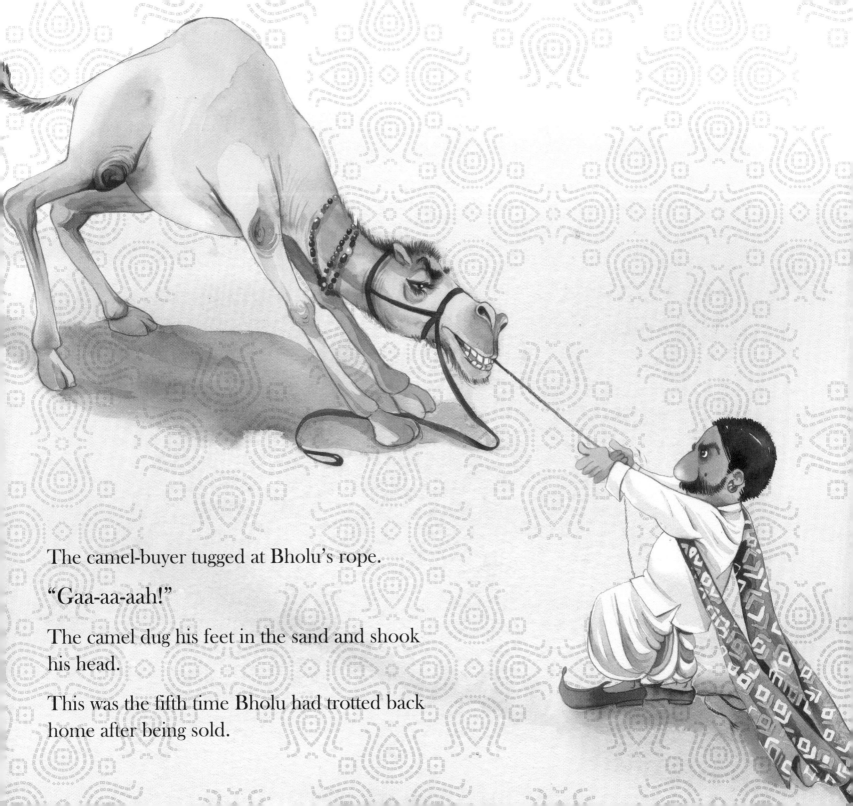

The camel-buyer tugged at Bholu's rope.

"Gaa-aa-aah!"

The camel dug his feet in the sand and shook his head.

This was the fifth time Bholu had trotted back home after being sold.

Beni Ram sighed.

"I'm sorry, sir," he said to the man. "He doesn't want to go with you. Here's your money back."

That night, Beni Ram and Bholu sat around a little bonfire.

"Bholiya," said Beni Ram, "The villagers use vans now instead of camel-carts. Nobody wants to give your old man a job any more."

The cold night air trembled as the old man's voice rose in song.

The starry desert skies echoed with the mournful humming of his sarangi.

Early next morning, three jeeps arrived from the next village.

Bholu stared at the people in colourful clothes, sun hats and sunglasses.

Everyone got onto camels, ready to ride into the open desert.

Everyone, except a little girl and her mother.

"I want to go on a camel ride too, Ma!" cried the little girl.

Mr Taparia looked worried.
"We are one camel short," he mumbled.

And then he spotted Bholu!

Bholu knelt down. The little girl and her mother climbed
onto his back.

The train of camels plodded across the golden sands.

Like a ship on the high seas, Bholu rocked and rolled.

The little girl squealed with excitement.

As the shadows grew longer, the men put up tents and lit lanterns.

Music filled the air. People sang and danced.

The song filled Bholu's heart with joy.

He lifted one leg and then the other. With every beat, the camel's hooves struck the sands. His long neck swayed to the rhythm.

The little girl joined in and danced with Bholu.

Everyone clapped.

"What would you like for a gift, my boy?" asked Mr Taparia, scratching Bholu's chin.

The camel pulled back his rubbery
lips in a big grin and looked towards
Beni Ram.

The next day, Beni Ram had
a new turban,
a new jacket with shiny mirrors,
new pointy shoes . . .

. . . and a new job!